Count from Zero to One Hundred

Alan Cunningham is a writer from the north of Ireland. Currently based in London, he was born in Newry and has previously lived in Belfast, Dublin and Berlin. He has taught on issues relating to appropriation and art at the Node Centre for Curatorial Studies, Berlin, and on Intellectual Property issues at Queen Mary, University of London. *Count from Zero to One Hundred* is his first book.

Count from Zero to One Hundred

Alan Cunningham

Penned in the Margins

LONDON

PUBLISHED BY PENNED IN THE MARGINS
Toynbee Studios, 28 Commercial Street, London E1 6AB
www.pennedinthemargins.co.uk

First published 2013

Printed by Bell and Bain Ltd, Glasgow

ISBN
978-1-908058-08-9

INTRODUCTION

Count from Zero to One Hundred is a personal declaration of bodily liberty and a reflection on the power of language and imagination to establish such liberty over and within the body. When I started writing what was to become *Count from Zero to One Hundred*, in 2010, I had yet to see any connection between what I understood it to be and the work of Kenzaburō Ōe regarding his relationship with his — as he terms him in *Rouse Up O Young Men of the New Age!* — 'handicapped son.'[1] I had two objectives in mind when I started.

First, I was half way through another still unfinished book, a novel laden with psychological complexity and a certain type of linguistic strictness, an historical novel that was becoming a bane upon my mental health. I found that I had stopped writing, and realized I needed both a break and a kick-start. Secondly, and as a result of a number of real life events, I realized that I was in desperate need of establishing some kind of psychologically healthy relationship with my body. Inspired, initially, by watching the film *Chungking Express*, (and by later finding out that the director, Wong Kar-wai, had shot the film very quickly and instinctively in response to his own difficulties during the editing of an historical epic, *Ashes of Time*), I decided to start writing every day about myself and my body in a contemporary and much more instantaneous and instinctive style.

It was only half way through the writing process of this new work that I was reminded of the work of Ōe by a friend. Sometime after this I then chanced upon a copy of *Rouse Up* in a second hand

---

[1] *Rouse Up O Young Men of the New Age*, Kenzaburō Ōe, Atlantic Books, London, 2002 (translated by John Nathan). All quotes from *Rouse Up* are from this edition.

bookstore in Berlin. Upon reading it I found that there were many similarities in theme. One section, in particular, affected me greatly.

Halfway through the book Ōe writes of how his wife turns to him one day and, having finished preparations concerning their handicapped son going to a job training center for the first time, says, 'I think I'll put Mr. F's pamphlet on the constitution in Eeyore's smock packet — that's sort of what he asked us to do.'

Returning to his study to find this pamphlet, Ōe is reminded of this Mr. F, an Okinawan native. He recalls a dinner at his own house where Mr. F refused to let Ōe's wife fall into depression and despair when considering the situation of her son. During the dinner, Ōe recalls, Mr. F abruptly said to her, 'Your boy's handicap doesn't seem that serious; if this were Okinawa, you could put him in a regular class.' In response to her saying that she and the other parents of handicapped children had only one thing in mind where ever they happened to be — 'living even one day longer than their child so they would always be there to care for them' — Mr. F then declared:

> 'Mrs! You mustn't think that way! That's defeatism! In the society we must create, your boy would carry this pamphlet in his shirt pocket, and whenever he had a problem he'd hold it up and say 'Look Here!' and the problem would go away! Anything less than that goal is defeatism!'

Ōe blends memories of Mr. F and the pamphlet with reflection on his unfinished goal of creating a 'collection of definitions for handicapped children relating to our world, society, and mankind, a project that was to include a retelling of the constitution in my own words for Eeyore's sake.' As *Rouse Up* progresses, however, the character of

Ōe realises that his goal is somewhat misguided and that in fact his son has as much to teach him as he can teach through any poetic re-telling of the Japanese Constitution. He writes

'Until now, it had been my goal to provide definitions of things and people for Eeyore's sake; but at this moment it was Eeyore, presenting me with a stanza from Blake's *Milton* as a lucid vision, who was creating a definition for his father:

Then first I saw him in the Zenith as a falling star
Descending perpendicular, swift as the swallow or swift
And on my left foot falling on the tarsus, enter'd there.'

Reading *Rouse Up*, I began to view the work I was engaged in as, in addition to its original purpose, a re-imagining of the poetic constitution that Ōe — as fictional father/narrator — considers writing. As Ōe writes about being inspired by William Blake and his *America, A Prophecy* (itself a poetic expression of the philosophy and principles of the U.S. Declaration of Independence), so I came to be inspired by Ōe and his thoughts of forming his own poetic take on the post-war Japanese Constitution.

The Constitution, enacted on the 3rd May 1947, famously contains an article — Article 9 — that actively renunciates the right of the state to wage war; it is also notable for Article 13 which states:

'All of the people shall be respected as individuals. Their right to life, liberty, and the pursuit of happiness shall, to the extent that it does not interfere with the public welfare, be the supreme consideration in legislation and in other governmental affairs.'

The Constitution was of particular importance to Okinawans, Okinawa having been placed under U.S. military jurisdiction for a period of 27 years after the end of World War II (there are still numerous U.S. military bases situated in the prefecture). During this time many Okinawans pointed to the new Japanese Constitution as a justification for complete Okinawan repatriation.

There is something else of note, however, which has led me to think that all the events occurring throughout the development of the work were, in some strange way, serendipitous. In 1981, in the no longer existent journal *Shin Okinawa Bungaku*, an anonymously written document was published, the author being identifiable only by the letter 'F'. This 'Unofficial Constitution of the Republic of the Ryukyus' was no doubt a reaction to the continued U.S. military presence on Okinawan land and inspired by the Ryukyuan independence movement (the Ryukyu islands are a chain of islands that include Okinawa). Two things stuck out upon reading the document (and thanks here must be given to John Purves, who provides an English translation of this document on his website http://www.niraikanai.wwma.net/index2.html). First, Article 1 states that 'The Republic of the Ryukyus is a democratic republic based on the foundations of love and labour. Sovereignty resides with the people in whom love and labour are born. The people of the Republic of the Ryukyus will exercise all powers of sovereignty according to the Constitution'. Second, the unofficial Constitution also includes an article renouncing war of any form.

~

Count from Zero to One Hundred is not directly connected with actual political issues or aspirations. However, in my shout out of pride, in my dismissal of the limits that have been set, without distinction, by nature upon us all, I find one can isolate a core set of principles that act as a basis for any poetic constitution for the self, and, by extension, any society of selves. I also find that they reflect, in a way, certain principles set out in both the Japanese post-war Constitution and the unofficial Constitution of the Republic of the Ryukyus, the first beloved by Mr. F, the second, perhaps, even written by him.

They are, I believe, the following: love, a certain type of love, not love as it is commonly understood, but, rather, as I adapt from Zweig in *Beware of Pity*, love as something 'unsentimental but creative. It knows its own mind, and is determined to stand by the sufferer, patiently suffering too, to the last if its strength and even beyond'; struggle — or work/labour; and, finally, the renunciation of war in favour of a personal combativeness, a struggle with oneself.[2]

However, it is, in the main, the thought of the personal reactions of the mysterious Mr. F to difference — perhaps we can indeed imagine him as the same 'F' who was the author of the unofficial Constitution — that inspired me to consider this work as a constitution of its own kind, an *Okinawan* Constitution, a declaration to myself concerning my relationship to the world. I hope it is read in the same spirit.

AC

---

[2] *Beware of Pity*, Stefan Zweig, Pushkin Press, London, 2011 (translated by Anthea Bell).

Acknowledgements

I would like to thank the following for their support of my writing, given both directly and indirectly, in more recent times and in times past: Noel, Esther, Darko, Jeroen, John, Bjarte, Gamal, Celeste, Jane, Paula V., the Altes Finanzamt collective in Berlin, Eirik, Joanna, Ian, Paula R., Barry, Noam, Florian, Sarmad, Alun, my parents, brother and sister and all those other friends and acquaintances who have heard me spin my tales of writing and publication over the years in Berlin and gave me some room, physical and otherwise, to get down to it. And particular thanks, of course, to Tom and Penned in the Margins.

The reference to the composer and the street cleaner in section 53 is based upon a tale recounted by conductor Arvo Pärt in an interview with *The Guardian* on 6th January 2011, 'Composer Arvo Pärt: Behind the beard.' Section 81 was inspired and influenced by a TMZ.com interview with Charlie Sheen on 28th November 2011.

Disclaimer

This is somewhat a work of fiction. Names, characters, places and incidents either are products of the author's imagination, somewhat, or are used somewhat fictitiously. Any resemblance to actual events or locales or persons, living or dead, is perhaps entirely coincidental, but then again, perhaps it is not.

Count from Zero to One Hundred

1

I was in Ireland and all I can remember thinking about was... I was in London and all I can remember thinking about was... I was in Berlin and all I was thinking about was... I was in a woman's bed and all I was thinking about was what I wanted.

I wanted anonymity, easily available through ignorance of language. What I really wanted — what that anonymity in fact was — was something more powerful, more destructive. I wanted erasure of my self, I wanted the result of choosing either to not remember or not learn the words with which we can communicate.

I wanted to cease to exist.

•

What had caused this desire to take hold of me? Well, many things, over the course of many years. And the gradual accumulation of those years into something called a life had hewn a sad strength out of me, had allowed me to forget about wanting to conclude an unfinished event.

But in that woman's bed, something happened, or I believed something to have happened. I'm not sure. Whether it happened or not doesn't matter. The act — seen, unseen, imagined, unimagined — brought that forgotten desire to the surface of my mind, and I thought again about what I had always wanted.

I wanted to cease to exist, to shout, to curse, to rage, to stop doing what I was doing and run out on to the streets and bang my head against the windows of the cars, to scream, cry, to do many, many other ridiculous and necessary things.

She had looked at me.

•

I had been looking too, of course. In Ireland. In London. In Berlin. In many other places. But the observation I had been engaged in was of a strange kind, quite unlike her act. It was a constant looking, not a looking at. It was driven by an indifference to response; by, perhaps, a reluctance for such a thing to happen.

I hadn't been looking at all.

•

Here is a bad day, but I do not want pity, please. I'm too strong for that now. I present it only as an indication of how far I have gone wrong. It is an attack on myself. You will surely think I am mad.

Imagine a gun, and imagine wanting to feel it against your head. You are not sure what will happen next. You only want the sensation, initially, the promise of a possible end to things. You are too vain, too lucky in other respects, to continue. But imagine that gun, and imagine wanting it at your head.

Before that, you feel like your head is going to explode, but you have no words for what you feel. You gesture and roam about your house, your apartment, the streets, you are tense, your arms move, you slap them together, you punch a fist into the palm of your other hand, or something like that, you feel shame, you want to leave, you wonder why you do these things to yourself, your body repels, you repel your body, you close your eyes, you grimace, you want to stop and ignore all existence, you tense your body in an attempt to reject, disappear, change the molecules, atoms, particles that surround you.

•

Let us try it another way. She told me she had looked at me. My head was lying in the space between her shoulder and her jaw, my lips touching her neck. My eyes were closed. I was soon glad they were closed. I was soon glad she couldn't see my face. She said, without moving,

"You know, I only really saw your other hand for the first time yesterday."

•

She was used to being looked at, and looking at others. She was what you might call 'good looking'. She dressed well. She had a good, wholesome body. She was a performance poet, she was a musician, she was an artist, she was an intelligent woman, she was stupid, she was Irish, she was Australian, she was confident, she did not understand.

This was in 2009. This was in Berlin. A world of my own making had collapsed, and so I had gone back.

2

Strong. I felt strong, being back. Weak, strong. I knew nothing, planned nothing, had no expectations. I felt ready for some kind of an ending. I moved into a ground floor apartment with a good friend. The place reeked of damp, clothes took weeks to dry, I got a cough, none of it bothered me. I worked, I was getting things done, the things I needed to do. We had good conversations. It seemed that he understood something and we didn't have to talk about that. I started to laugh again, silly things were said over the dinner table and I could almost feel the tension easing in my body.

•

I believe I've had that tension all my life, that it was a necessity for survival, an ability to resist, to take some kind of punishment and still function. I believe my body remembers what happened, that first organic shock when things stopped happening as usual and whatever is expected suffered a deviation. The body reacts, the body will always react, blood flows differently, ounces, quarts, cells, numbers are known as wrong, something snaps in the brain and the child, with no words, no way of telling, reacts in only one way, the only way. A resistance. My mind, my body, they have continued since then — how could they not? What I thought of as normal is not, in fact, a regular occurrence. Such things are the act of a man remembering pain, and a life beginning to change, or stop, or something like that. Such things are the act of a body that had to resist, that resisted something horrible, something unknown, unseen, but remembered. Such things are not usual.

•

While we are fucking, when she comes, she tightens her legs around my ribcage, slight, lean, and she squeezes as if she wants to break me and I think something is going to break and then she pushes her head onto mine and pushes and pushes and all I can feel is her skull, the hard bone of it and I know then that I want all of this, only all of this. I want her to break it all. Break it, I think, and crack my skull for good measure, I will not mind.

We speak only German.

She makes me laugh.

We talk simply, about food, some books, funny words. She seems to understand something and we don't have to talk about that.

•

"Are you afraid?"

"No."

"Of nothing?"

"Nothing."

"Of losing nothing?"

"No."

It has become a dangerous time for me. My answers are truthful. Maybe that frightens me? I think about that for a second, then disregard it. I am not frightened. I have begun to accept something, but I worry now, if I accept, will things fall apart? Warmth is given, and warmth is offered in return, but I am still resistant. The body remembers; the mind, it serves the body.

3

I start to shake — my whole body shakes — after I have written down something true. Things are falling apart, perhaps, my body knows, is constantly prepared, the shaking is a sign, things must be wrapped tighter, must be made more secure. I remember this shaking, something from my youth, unexplainable.

She said that I shook while I slept next to her; that I shook violently.

4

The shaking will not stop. A highly tensile body has been the only constant of my life. Relaxation — acceptance — may be an apocalyptic act. Relaxation brings to the body the memory of: potential death, the victory of deformity.

•

Be careful of women bearing gifts, but be careful of it as a man, because you are a man, because of what you are, for men want only praise and warmth, and you, because of your body, want it more than most.

Warmth is misleading, warmth is that drug which promised to someone else an easing of pain, the pain of formation, a proper pain, and that is why it attacked the body, because that body wanted cruelty, it needed it, needs it still. It rejected the easing of pain. My body was an anti-body to that drug, whatever it was called. Perhaps the body got what it wanted, the other — being whole — may have been more torturous than I can imagine. Warmth eases life. My body remembers, the mind... yes, it serves the body still.

•

She sees in me something fictional, I believe, what she wants to see, I look good — she does not yet know all of me — and that appeals to her, she likes good-looking things, aesthetics, as she terms it. I can delude her for a while, I don't need to advertise such things, I have the face for it, I suppose, and the words, yes, especially the words, and she likes words too, strange that, my face, young face, grey hair.

I maintain her fiction, let her believe it. I like being found attractive. Eventually we acknowledge the need to touch, my body remembers, my mind serves my body. She is offering me something, it relaxes me, but I am afraid, I am worried, she does not yet know all of me. She offers me tobacco and cigarette papers, an offer that I, confused — surely she must have seen by now? — politely turn down.

5

And here is warmth: she pulled a pink dress down over her head and her body and shook out her hair as it reappeared into the morning. I playfully mocked the action, making it into a bad advertisement, and she stuck her tongue out at me, smiling, before disappearing into the bathroom.

There is no redemption, but I must remember to let my body be touched.

6

Before you, beside you, under you, on you, lies, works, moves, sleeps: the body of a beautiful woman. Are you looking at that body, what do you see, what do you make of it? More than you can make of your own. Never properly born, like the man said. *Liebst du noch?* You go to bed with a beautiful, sexy woman, just like John said, and you don't have sex with her? Are you alive?

They have their own thoughts on the matter, of course. Their bodies, viewed just as yours can be. Bloat. Fleshy arse. Big, chunky thighs. Tired eyes. Belly. Not so bad, that, perhaps. Bad hair. Puff. Sag. Big fat fingers. Nose, ears, lips, feet. Old neck. Age. How old are you? You should never ask. Even the beautiful ones fade, you see things you never imagined. What parts are pure, what can be left alone from assessment? Not much, maybe.

She is beautiful, but it is only beauty, beauty nonetheless.

•

"Show 'er, Show 'er."

Gamal, excited by our earlier conversation, during which truths were uttered, or heard from somewhere, or felt because of something, pizza, perhaps, or vodka and syrup, provokes me.

And so I do as he asks, laughing, no, smiling, not laughing, he is laughing, and illuminating the conversation we — she and I — are having with some kind of rawness. Because of our earlier conversation, because of a freedom I feel that night, I show her. And, it appears as if she had known all along, she reacts with a nonchalance — beauty, again — that annoys, no, not annoys, disarms me. She found me beautiful and kind, she told me, what does the rest of it matter, but I wasn't convinced, I pressed the matter, whereupon she proclaimed it, ignored it, was eventually exasperated by my obsession and walked off, not angrily, just so, leaving me with my looking, looking, looking, and my not looking at.

•

She, another, tended to me, mother-like, and that was what I liked.

She, another, we fucked, only.

7

No, not fuck, only.

•

There was, perhaps, some kind of recognition. Here it goes:

I, running up steps, thinking, why not run down, why not walk back to her? I was lonely, I needed help. I could give her recognition in return for help. I don't know. We sat on the cold steps of an U-Bahn station and kissed, I probably told her she was beautiful. I was happy to. She knows what she was thinking.

Returning from a trip to London, I discovered that she had organised things. Work had been done in my apartment, astonishing me. This was always the way, she was happy to help, I was happy to let her feel wanted, when she wanted it. She once tied my undone shoelace in Rose's. She bought me things if I mentioned that I needed them, not meaning it. A gift of boiled eggs and bread for a trip to Ireland. I must put more stock in my words, in what people take from them.

I failed to recognise her one day, when she sat down opposite me and ordered a coffee.

•

I moved on to other things. The shape of a woman's back, a strong arm.

Penetrative sex. Strange, when she told me that she and her old boyfriend hadn't had it for six years, my first thought was confusion, my second a kind of happiness. Woman sees cock in her, feels it, sees her cunt round cock, sees cunt, cock, man sees cock in woman, feels it, asks her to feel it whilst inside, talking, squeeze my balls, can't wait to feel you entering me, she says, both see themselves reflected, hear themselves, through the other's eyes, ears. Movement, pleasure, pain, control. A question of power.

No longer important.

•

Jess tells me she finds her old art tutor attractive, tells me that he once killed a cat to make an artistic point. I object.

"Don't be so conservative, so moral."

"It's not being moral, I'm being ethical, very different thing. What I believe doesn't come from somewhere else. It's a problem with power being imposed on something powerless. It's a question of how we interact with the circumstances of our existence."

•

I get horny, sure, but the thought of having sex with her once more fills me with a visceral nausea. I don't want to lose myself in a body anymore, in the body of another.

•

There is some sense in the nonsense. There is a reason, like Jeroen said, for something to happen, but it's not a oneness I'm worried about, not an idea of oneness that cannot survive, but rather that around the two, the three, the everybody, some space gets connected, and once connected no space is left for the just one, the just two. Air gets commingled. It becomes impossible to remove oneself without difficulty, the space is joined to other space, not the body to the body, nor the mind to the mind.

The atoms, molecules, particles around me are changing, I believe, mixing, it is something unstoppable, a simple operation of nature. I move in my space, the other body in another, the space adjoins. The body remembers, the mind serves the body, space surrounds all, all is subject to space.

•

Let us consider other things.

First, movement. There's a disgrace felt in movement, so much so that I have developed what can only be referred to as poise, but in the privacy of a room, even with clear, open windows, I can dance without reflection and clap and look at myself. I might even take a photograph of it all.

But then I don't want to be seen anymore. I don't need to be.

•

The space around us is startled, it drags my body into a meeting with another. This, I think, is a good thing. Thankful for air, for molecules, heat, power, atoms, gravity, my body is then not thankful, then thankful, only memory rejects this movement, but the movement is a kind one, I think, or, at least, one that cannot easily be avoided if one is said to be still alive.

Be satisfied with your own life, your own body. Why do you want the life of another? I don't, but the molecules are changing, colliding in space, I hadn't asked them to. Everything serves space.

This is what space is:

hair that, a smell of something, something that turns the brain off, that makes the eyes roll back, skin that, touch, grabbing, the want to touch, the need to, the dragging of a hand over a back, a simple finger, talk, laughter, easy laughter, laughter in eyes, the something that drags the flesh together in a way that does not disrupt existence, legs that break, the muscle that draws the eye and encourages a bite.

She has a body, but it is only a body, a body nonetheless.

8

There is only recognition of bodies and of pain. There is a delusion that there is a way, dissolve ourselves in another body and mind, I, more than most, would like this, but I cannot, I have to keep my body, work it, feel it, watch it collapse in on itself. I want dissolution, of course I want to forget, she says things that mirror Joyce and the blind man, but it only frustrates me, difference is only interesting to the sane and the whole, dissolution to the insane, the unwholesome.

9

I become bold, no longer any thoughts regarding how consequences relate to the past. An autumnal cooling is occurring, my body is cooling, the blood had been raised in temperature, had been raised to the very surface, an action inspired by memory and circumstance, no doubt, and now it is cooling down, which appears to be in accordance with things.

I will have to let the body be drawn out.

•

Outside, walking, I think about desire. I have it no longer, and yet I am attracted to it, when I see it in others. Perhaps that's a lie. I have desire, I just have no inspiration. Warmth, she said, and that has something of the ring of truth to it, perhaps, and then I start to think of fire, and silence drawn out with others, but it was a comfort, there was no aspiration, at least for me, aspiration ignores the world, ignorance, just as bad, condemns it.

•

I'm thinking of a proper story for you now, I realise you are tiring, you need to be entertained, something will occur to me, patience, patience. Some kind of story of the outside, of being in the outside, feeling the cold, in autumn, winter, but enjoying the effect of that on the body, recognising it as essential. A story of the outside.

10

Perhaps this (although it is the story of another):

And now I must show... what? The air has become mixed. I breathe that of another. The body serves space, the mind decides how to follow.

Whether to follow.

This is not the story of another.

11

I walk. Not during the day. In the daytime I sleep, or watch movies, or write while lying in the bed. The window of my room opens onto the courtyard and I am reluctant to pull back the blinds that cover it, not only because I want privacy but also — more so — because I am now afraid, no, not afraid, perhaps, but rather somewhat sensitive to the light. Has this been caused by my time in that other world, the world that collapsed around me, the world that I dismantled? I am not sure, but I know that when I leave the house, it is usually dark, and I feel happy, there is no light in the air that my body needs to react against.

•

I walk to parties, openings, readings, meetings with friends, meetings with people I have an interest in fucking, meetings with people I have no interest in fucking, and while I walk I enjoy the movement of my body, and perhaps this is why I enjoy the dark, I think, because I cannot be properly seen.

While I walk I think about:

we drive to Belfast, she and I, and I suppose there is something of an expectation in the car, I have not thought about the matter, it hasn't even been discussed, the appropriateness of it, so I think, now, writing this now, there was an expectation. That drive, that journey, was, in some way, the thing to be done. I believe there was an expectation that to do things in another way would not be the way to go about them, but yet, which of us could have known that? (And yet, I think now, that is the way things have gone. Your body knows.)

This was when the roads that took one to Belfast were constructed — much as they are now, perhaps — as if pointing to the promise of destruction: they drew the car in, and caught it up in a maze of aggression and confusion, no map, no plane upon which to discover longitude or latitude. There were corners and entries and exits of which few had explicit knowledge and all you could do was prepare for their possibility, and not be shocked by what developed.

The hospital is surrounded by Nissen huts, and has a military wing, protected, corrugated, and we must drive in such a way that the limits to our freedom are made clear — but this is nothing new to me.

The hospital then: water, calcium sulphate hemihydrate, a tight fitting around that which is left, a hardening, the creation of a vacuum of little air inside so that when all is finished there is a satisfying heft to the thing as that which was planned, which was expected, is pulled off, and that, that *smell*, of what?

•

We are outside, we are leaving, the skin on my arm itches, I brush — what? — something off and look, to my left, at the architecture of decay and defence but again, it doesn't shock me and it was then, I think, that I realised that this was the place for my body to grow, that elsewhere I would have only softened.

12

Jess arrives at the apartment, the new apartment where I am temporarily living. It is an apartment of great light and it is elevated. The effect of all this on my body is disconcerting. I have much less energy than some months before.

She is distraught, a little drunk. She bemoans the sad cases that she has just seen on the U-Bahn. She imagines that it is not the case that someone, that many, has, have, ever talked about the misery and poverty constantly seen in parts of the city.

She talks with anger about men with no teeth, men with beards who chomp and gristle, the lame, and I suddenly realise she is very afraid. Perhaps it is understandable, I think: there was a recent unwelcome encounter with a man one night before, and a moment where he — drunk, confused, flush — offered her money at the door of her building.

I realise she is frightened, want to pull off my jumper, shoes, everything, bare myself to her and say: something, I don't know what.

13

I begin to plan for something. I want to bring something to the world, but am not quite sure what. I purchase the necessary materials, drafting paper, pencils, and start to work.

14

I asked her if she could roll me a cigarette. She was fire, dark eyes and beautiful, pale skin, an Italian nose, Persian hair, red lips.

She asked me why I couldn't roll my own, why I wanted her to do it, was it some kind of male trip?

I said no, offered her proof of my inability, looked into those dark eyes with ease. Let her speak, look straight into her eyes, you believe her. Trust me. Some sign of madness there, I thought. She may have thought the same. She wanted to struggle with me, but I didn't want to fight, I offered her grace. At this point in time, I still had no desire.

And something took off in her, I couldn't exactly understand it. Was she angry with me for my acceptance, my... what?

She said that I wasn't a man, that I had no feelings, she railed against me as we three walked to another bar, and then I simply took off across the street as she ranted, alone, unable to put up with — no, not unable to put up with, merely tired with — her list of complaints. After her flatmate and I fucked some weeks later, for the second time, the flatmate told me that she had mentioned our situation to the woman of power, had been answered with a very simple: "I don't want to talk about that."

And now I think that what she said was true: I cannot feel anything.

15

In the new world, in a new world, but still the world, I thought I was going mad and no doubt I was.

I questioned things, I don't know why, and such questions were not answered, were unanswerable, or considered not important by those with whom I was in love.

It was then — again, I have no doubt — that she began to see me clearly.

•

I moved to a city in the north, close to the water, humid, moved through the land by train, seeing only desiccated cows and salt.

In that small city I was able to mix and not fear the weight of history, nor fear the weight of my own body. I played card games and learned the value of patience. There was no more judgment. I thought I began to understand. I heard stories of love lost, stories of the world and children mourned, drunks who wanted to fight because they were sad, and I saw the full girth of the world and our struggle within it.

I don't know if I saw any of these things.

16

I am overwhelmed by the air around me, it changes, takes on a form related to yours, but it is only a memory of your form.

It envelops me.

I caress it.

17

I sit down at a desk in a room and begin to think about things I do not understand.

In the middle sit those things which root us to some place, grass which I want to walk upon, rain which falls upon me, distracting me from feelings of neglect, the sun, making me afraid or drawing me out of myself, objects I can only see the light of, things which make me feel small, water, salt, light which I look at and which makes me think about destruction.

Around this are other things. Streets, cobbled, they are only constructions, things that can easily be changed. Tall buildings, windows to be looked into, windows to be ignored, the worry of money, a drink, a cigarette, many people. Walking, traveling at great speeds under, over, around. Working, not working, eating, looking. Looking most of all, and looks at and to, and listening.

A punch in the face. An unpleasant stare. A stare of desire.

Sleeping in beds that are not one's own.

18

Part of me still longs for sickness when I feel it coming upon me, when I meet friends in cafés and I can see their faces puffed and red with the stinking fluid of illness. When I feel my throat get sore. Then I remember the night when I broke my hand against a wall. Some thought it was a romantic act, I told most people I had fallen off my bicycle, but I remember clearly what she said to me and how happy I was when the bone connected with concrete and I felt that pain — it had the comfort of the familiar — which reminded my body that something very clearly had gone wrong.

The breaking of the bone was necessary, a return to first principles.

People looked at it and thought I didn't need to see a doctor, but I knew that I had to go. I remembered.

•

I realised then that strength was important to me and that without it, well...

19

Why must I write all of this down? Why can I not simply eat, fuck, sleep, work at something and laugh?

Tomorrow, I will stop writing.

Tomorrow, I will begin to make money again and I will give all that I make to those whom I love.

But the thought of such an act scares me, and I realise again that the woman of power was right: I cannot feel anything.

•

I must stop talking about all these complications. Why don't you simply shut your mouth and fuck her like she wants you to? What is wrong with you?

•

I walk home from a night out during which a girl looks at me and I just carry on smoking my cigarette thinking about what she has seen, what she believes she has seen. She wants me to look back, is waiting for it, and I offer it to her as a gift, without arrogance, with peace, a vindication of her body and her eyes, yes, of course you are attractive but then I keep looking and I make it clear that all of that is not enough, not exactly what I am looking for. I turn away, without smiling, without talking, happy to smoke a cigarette in my own company and I realise she still stares and all I can think about is: what exactly are you looking for?

•

I walk home in the rain, cursing myself, my stupidity, the water seeps into my shoes, I cannot afford to have them resoled just yet, I cannot afford to buy new shoes.

20

She wakes in the early morning and tells me that I do not shake any more and I think this is perhaps a good thing, something desirable.

I think about returning to the house that my parents live in, something has to be communicated and quickly. I remember previous conversations where I learnt that pain is not exclusive to the self, I learnt that blame is a function of our existence and then there were tears and I realised that something had been communicated, over years, only not with words. Only acts of love. Because of this I had not seen it.

Body, again, softness is impossible, it only wants to cut, crunch, starve, fatten, lean, it cannot simply connect, there is no comfort there or it is the comfort of − is comfort as − an imminent disaster, a sign.

Absence, money earned, travel. I begin to remember more clearly, not seeing only words.

Think.

I see: no, I still cannot see it, I am full of disgust, there is no hope, no hope for me.

21

Something had happened to my body, something that was now being rectified. I had run it, starved it, purified it out of all ability and now, being back, I needed to burn it a little, to jump start it through dissolution back into some kind of living.

•

I go walking, thinking about coffee and how little it affects me nowadays, sure in the knowledge that it must be affecting me but understanding that something in me is not affected, something has left me, worry, perhaps, or, late enough, I have learned that I can still function nonetheless.

I see what I believe to be a woman coming out of a cafe, putting into her mouth and lighting a cigarette, her hair is pulled back tight and the skin is now orangey brown, make up, and the eyes black, and there is a toughness there, but as she gets closer she sees my look, worries, but it is only a look of affection: it is the only look I have.

She looks down, momentarily nervous, and then I see those signs that would confuse others, a darkness beneath make up, a squareness, but I am not confused, my affection remains and I want to look into those eyes and offer some comfort — trust me — but looking at is a dangerous thing, another is always looked at, another always looks, or does not, back.

22

What would it be like to be in a strong land, you think, as you lie down and try to sleep, try to stop that heart pounding, a land where people are strong, fit, healthy and whole, and you would pretend that you are like them all, everyone would pretend, but you are not, you realise, you simply want an approving gaze, and you are not even sure you want that.

•

As you lie there you think about what it is you feel you have to say, why you feel you cannot say it in the company of others, why you fear being known, knowing that you are known, knowing that it is all so obvious, fearing the breakdown of your body, the gaze of the eye that sees you and knows you and:

she did not know you, she saw you as she wanted to, as you presented yourself to her, which was what you believed she wanted, what all want, but yet you could be comfortable around her, it was not that, it was her fear of the gaze of others, that was what caused you to decay, her fear — you saw it — of being completely herself and then you realise that this, this fear, is what you fear of others, because you cannot understand it:

you know exactly what you are, what you are capable of, what you are incapable of and that gives you grace, you do not feel the need to be otherwise, you have no choice, it can all be seen, others can hide too easily, their bodies allow them that, and that makes you fearful, that they cannot really be seen, that they will change what is in the mind, but their bodies will stay the same, beautiful, capable of convincing you, you cannot convince with your body, it is all to easy to see that you are broken down, a wreck, incapable of the poise you always affect.

•

As you begin to feel that you are sleeping, you think: in that strong land your mind is seen as a deformity, but your mind is clear, you are not lying and your body can never be untruthful.

23

You have got to claim it — Do you even hear the call of it? Can you not see the beauty of it? — as your own. Look now, be alive, do not let a dream of what you think is needed distract your body from what it is.

24

"Fuck off."

My first reply to the question, the always asked question:

"What happened..?"

"Do you mind if I..?"

"Can I ask you a personal..?"

Of course not. Impose your self upon my body, vocalise your gaze, your questioning, curious gaze. You have looked, why shouldn't you speak? What harm could be done?

•

A child will look and ask the question innocently, with a certain amount of disgust, or at least horror, the horror of recognising that something is not right, not quite within their realm of known experience, and this I prefer, because the reaction is truthful, it vindicates my own feeling about myself. The questions of adults allow me to wallow in a dream of equanimity, whereas what I am really thinking, what they are really thinking is: thank God...

•

The question of the child makes me happy because it returns me to my body, it reminds me that I am pretending, that the pose is not quite working...

25

I will make my body known, and I will know it too. If I am tied to it, if I cannot unfix what is seen, how it is seen, then I must refuse the desire for anonymity that comes from fear, I will refuse to go unnoticed. I reject nausea, I reject contempt, I reject hatred, the shaking, the trembling, the fear, the sickness and I reject the shame.

•

You disgust yourself, you are unsure of what to do with it, others have clear options, everything for you is a new construction, a mapping of dangerous currents that, you believe, have the potential to wash you away from everything good and clean and proper if you do not have an idea of how your body must be.

•

You know what you can do and what you cannot but the gaze questions everything and this makes you unsure of how to continue, for to continue and to fail, or even falter, is to vindicate the gaze, but you know what you can do... for someone with... with, with what?... well... you do very well...

26

I had been looking for nothing at all. I needed to remain in contact with people. I could not do without it. I couldn't pretend to be strong any more, I couldn't offer that to anyone. I wanted to revel in my weakness. I didn't want to be a man.

I could go no further with things. When something is offered, my reaction is crooked, somehow most definitely wrong.

27

Jess calls and wants to talk. I walk to her house, up the stairs and she makes me coffee with milk and brandy. She cried the night before, she's worked herself up into a state about this guy, and she explains it to me, the nausea, sickness, and I try to be rational and try to explain it to her, tell her to be patient but there are complications, it's never easy and though he likes her, feels the connection, there are other things and you need that body like a newborn needs its mother, like... that. Who knows how it happens. That's the sickness.

28

Talking to her, I slowly start to realise that she is very much herself when she is at home — when she is at that place where she grew, where important parts of her development took place. Well, I think, as much as anybody can be themself in such a place. But in that place where she is supposed to be herself — where one believes it is allowed, if no where else, where it should be allowed — she does it. She smokes, drinks, behaves — so I imagine — as she always does, anywhere else. There is no artifice.

You, on the other hand, you think, are not yourself — cannot, in fact, be yourself — when you are at home, at that place where you grew, it always seems completely impossible for that to happen, there is always judgment — by you and by others — and yet...

•

"I need warmth", she whispers into your ear, "I need talk, I need intimacy, I need a body, I need to laugh."

•

You begin to feel a certain type of nervous dread, you realise that you have started to think about the future again, after a time when you have been very content — when it has been healthy for you — to completely disregard the very idea of the future, the very idea of a past. Current time begins to move in relation to other things, other times. This is what makes you fearful, the idea that you have some perspective that is helpful. Something in you knows that it is the idea of a fool.

29

"We're not immortal", she says, sounding almost shocked at what she has said, and what caused her to think it, at the realisation of this, the most empirical of truths. I want to laugh, but that is not appropriate, I think: then, I think, those would be her words, they are not yours.

•

I get too familiar with a body, fucking becomes comfortable, what would one say? Intimacy has been achieved. Dangerous, that. You begin to — perhaps it is not your mind, perhaps it is instinct, perhaps she even wants it that way — think of that body as your own. You want to possess it, own it, inhabit it and do with it what you will, like... like a newly purchased house. This is why you start to watch what she does with her body; how she puts her make up on, the boots she wears, her underwear. You feel that this body is your body, or that you would like it to be your body, if such a thing were possible. So you look with more consideration, you continue to fuck and the fucking becomes better, more intimate, and you begin to think: am I fucking her to become her? You begin to believe that you know what she thinks, why she does a thing, not a thing, but: it is not your body. Remember the presence of your own, you remind yourself, even if you hate it and it will fail you.

30

"I'd like to take a bath with you."

"There's a bath in my new place."

"Is it big?"

"Big enough for two people who want to take a bath together."

●

I have become a little sick of words, sick of the ability they have of appeasing something in us that would be better left unsatisfied.

●

I talk to Rachel about how I feel about unhappiness, about how I believe that happiness never — now, more than ever — feels quite real, I always believe that it is a story I have convinced myself I should believe even as it is happening, even as I am thinking, yes, this could be happiness and as I am talking to her and explaining my philosophy I start to realise that perhaps I am just uncomfortable being happy, that happiness does not help me nor my body. I realise that my philosophy is not real, it is only something I believe to make me feel better about things, it is what I do to make myself happy. Will I only be happy knowing — believing that I know — everything that will ever happen to me?

•

She tells me about this new boy she is seeing. He asked her to be his girlfriend. After an initial agreement, she later changes her decision — correctly, I stupidly think to myself — to decline his offer.

31

Let me be a body and let that body direct its energy appropriately. Do not burden — do not confuse — my mind with words, with meaningless words, or, if words are to be used — if it is that they must be — let them be completely new words, fit for new purpose, my purpose, my body.

32

I read some of my words on a radio show and I think: what awful rubbish it is you write, what awful shite. Why can't you be funny? Funny, I think, is never as easy as it looks. There is something to work at.

•

She tells me a story she has written, a story about the end of something, love, perhaps, she might believe that, but the story is not really about that, it becomes clear, the story is about, I think, the gifts we give, the gifts we believe we should give, when a gift is felt to be desired and it is about what we think they mean. The story is about a gift she gave to someone who liked hearts, the image of hearts — not the real image, you understand — but that image, that idea of a heart as something rounded, soft, only red and without, I think, any real character, whatever that might be.

She gifted him hearts of all description because she felt it was what he wanted. He — ready to wait, to continue to imagine — returned one of them to her, loaded with a significance that was not at all real and which makes me instantly think of the following words, no, not the words, but what they pointed to: fat, muscle, purple, white, frightening and life.

33

There is something wrong with me — no, now, come on, not wrong, think clearly — not wrong, I am not wrong. I do not want to be with another that doesn't act to — will not act to — satisfy my desire, but it is the desire that is wrong, the idea that there is something for me. I need to create — create, create — something else, some new words, entirely of — entirely for — my person.

•

But this acts to deny life, surely? But then what is deny, what am I denying? It is not to deny at all.

•

Softness makes me sick, I think, I forget myself, how my body works, which foods suit, in a room full of pleasures, losing myself in a body again. Because at times I do not want to be alone? Because pleasure makes me forget what it is to be alone, makes me forget that pleasure? She writes words on different parts of my body, words worthy of ridicule, "protection", "warmth" "strength", and I think she is mad, she is trying to write me, she is writing me as she sees me, I am not warm, I cannot protect, I am not strong.

•

She makes to write "strength" on the same arm where she has

written "warmth", a little higher up, and then she stops, moves to the other arm, and I think: what exactly are you doing, are you blind? Why would you pretend such a thing? She continues, irrespective. Language creates the event of her choosing. The tip of the marker traces, slowly, the blemish of a letter, then letters — the blemish of a word onto my skin. She smiles, unaware of my reluctance to agree, and holds my arm as she writes. I find it difficult to struggle. As I say, she sees what she wants to see, but...

I felt more peace when she was lying face down on the bed, naked, expectant, waiting for me to slap her, "hard", she said, "harder than that", I said, when she did the same to me, thinking that it would hurt, thinking that she had given me all she could. She hadn't, but I felt content all the same.

•

She acts to please, reacts — only ever in a way that she believes to be harmonious — to surroundings. I eat — have always only eaten — with a fork, she starts to eat only with a fork, but it nauseates me, this attempt — I don't care whether it is something that has been thought out or not — at what she believes to be some kind of calm. When she eats with only the fork, it looks so clumsy, she is clearly uncomfortable and I want to say: why aren't you using — as you so often do — a knife?

•

I tell her I don't want to be in Berlin at that moment, I want to be in

Ireland. It seems that I have the desire to dream again, how did I cut myself off from everything once more?

34

Someone dies.

•

I did not — still do not — know this person well, things, of course, would be different if that had been — if that were — the case, but it is not and so... I think about disease and the body against us, against what we think — but more so feel — is true.

I do not yet feel fear — why should I? — but something else, a something close — I believe — to that weakness which — to which — (that person who is now dead) succumbed, sometimes I am — not feel — so weak in life I think, yes, this must be — what? — but it is something else, not fear, no, but knowledge, no, not knowledge, yes, but memory, yes, a memory of — from? — my body, a weakness that — some gift — foreshadows.

The idea that — it is not even an idea, it is a fact, yes, I think, I am not — finally — afraid of facts — that body is around us, around mind, which does not — finally — work, that it can, and will, and must, turn, over time, what is our mind against, which finally does not work, this is something that is forgotten, but I have not forgotten, no, I — in fact — can not forget, I will only ever be a body, I am not around my body, I am nothing close to what I think I am, I am nothing that I want to be.

•

That dead person has written on her Facebook page

"Looks like an inflammation in my chest... what can I say?... it fucking aches"

and

"from chest pains to inflammation to a lung infection?... come on... whatever is happening to my body give it a rest... please..."

•

I remember the sensation of pain and I think of hope and — finally — I look at my body.

•

I think back to when I arrived back, remember how I decided — maybe not — to push my body in a direction that I had previously decided — absolutely — to ignore, certain elements, I thought, were missing and I was no longer properly configured — yes — for a life of imagination. I needed to ignore — what was it Blake said? — the idea of God. Beer, and fat, cheese and bread, mayonnaise, cigarettes. A modicum of (what is the opposite of health?).

35

Think of the body of a man amongst those of many women. They want to be — do they not? — looked at, to be loved, regarded both with affection and desire, and with joy, admired from far and near, adored and — dare I say it — beatified.

What was it she said? Everything is better with a woman around. But she meant only her.

•

The man reacts accordingly, there is — in fact — nothing to be done, the body is manipulated by certain elements of which nobody knows anything worth knowing, the women believe they want nothing, the man believes he acts of his own accord, or not, or something like that...

•

With circumstances reversed — woman, men — everything is precisely the same.

36

And then I think about, or — rather — my body is struck by how words make love, or love makes words which make love, or something like that, but something does happen, there are effects, and a body, existent or not, sleeps beside another without disruption to sleep, or eats in front another without disruption of digestion, or laughs, grunts, moans, cries in front of another with out something of something, or not, and even wants to be around that other body — and resolutely not — but wants to come back and can, will, be around that other body, and will sleep again, and will touch, and want to fuck, and not fuck, and not anything, and will want to be just a body, or, what it thinks, a body beside another body.

•

And then I think of a new word, or try to, and then, thinking of how my body acts, reacts, I laugh.

37

I go to a reading. I have been asked to write something relating to the year 1993, to which request I have agreed, but I find that I cannot — can no longer — motivate myself to write any words about this year, I cannot write down any words I believe have come — once they are read back — from my mouth. I think: if I cannot believe they have come from my mouth, no one will regard them once I say them out loud. My body will not convince them. I write something regardless, words are easily manipulated to present to listeners the appearance of meaning, listeners who expect meaning will construct meaning, even if there is no meaning. I read — my hand shakes, I start to move my legs, I almost start to walk — and someone takes — without asking for permission — a photograph of me.

•

The photograph arrives in my mailbox the next day, along with a number of others. I find my appearance in one photograph satisfying, in another revolting.

•

Without the vindication, the distraction of another body, I start to — or perhaps it is just the result of having drunk too much coffee — question my own, I see only weakness and crave a starvation of my stomach.

38

This is what happens to a body which is a deviation. The world is seen — negotiated — in a way different to most. Clumsy, and everything gets destroyed, I do not — can never — have the correct hold on things.

•

Your own advice, to avoid maintaining, or allowing, a relationship with distance, is perhaps — upon reflection — wrong, distance is the more desirable way to go, for there one can avoid the body altogether, and any obligations that are created, the impositions that our bodies make, the crush, the walk, the swell of, that inherent quality of judgment. Only with bodies do we have judgment.

•

Words push against the body, the cruelty of our bodies, love, some kind of love, is more revenge, it seems, imagination acts against our bodies, and what they have been designed, or rather not, to do.

39

And of course she is her own body, has fucked, kissed, penetrated in ways unimaginable to you, been penetrated by, been taken, been held, beholden, laughed, smiled, has bedazzled, been dazzled by, understood others, many others, kissed again, and your body is a something, a nothing to that, you cannot convince yourself of any significance, do not give your body a significance it does not have, but — please, please — do not undermine what it also is, what luck.

40

Out of necessity, on a aeroplane — for the first time in a long time — I try to do nothing, only emanate a desire to embrace all flesh that is comforting, so that I think less about my own.The aeroplane starts to move quickly along the runway. I try to do nothing, only... I close my eyes and place my head back against the headrest. I look to my left, at the carpet and at my neighbour. I look away from the window that I sit beside. My neighbour is large and something about that comforts me. I try to do nothing, only...The aeroplane escapes gravity, reaching, reaching; beneath us there is now the absence of some usual heaviness and soon there is a pain as some pressure tries my flesh. I try to do nothing, only emanate a desire to be embraced by comforting flesh. Then, something happens: some memory appears and becomes, impossible, yes, but a spirit — I know — but not like the one I imagined — remembered — earlier that morning. It is not at all frightening, no, my mind and my body appear to be in a much less frenzied place, on an aeroplane, of all places, and, with that spirit in front of me, my imaginings, rememberings, they sooth whatever ails me, I choose — it is no choice — to allow my body to be enveloped by something other than my mind, by another body, or, rather, the simple memory of that joy.

41

What is it about a woman, or a man, that brings full joy in me, if joy is felt, and makes me want to touch fingers that are not always there, or kiss lips that do not, in fact, exist.

•

Eyes lead somewhere, be open to all bodies, all embraces, be open to touch.

•

I damage the world – jumpers get torn as I take them off, fingers are cut, buttons pop, trousers are ripped, shoes lose their purchased glory — and think, why, why, am I careless still, or, perhaps, the world, this world, was not made in the image of anything I can understand, my body being here is, instead, an accident, I am, therefore, brusque, I break things and think nothing of it because that is my place in the world, while others look on, slightly disgusted.

•

Things are closed and I would prefer them to be always open but people cannot see this. In any event, that is the world.

42

I go to Stockholm, to London, to Melbourne, South Armagh, Berlin. I study — with little real enthusiasm — the Law, I teach English to businessmen and -women and to schoolchildren, I try to escape from the difficult act of creating a world, new words which I can understand and which point to something I can believe I have said, something which does not sicken me, which suits my body. I make an attempt to become a curator of art. I am frightened, I have little to say, there is nothing said or written which, I find, is expressed with much beauty, no, not beauty, but with simple and correct grammar.

•

In Ireland, I begin to realise what the difficulty is: people are pressing into taxis, while the taxi-man waits, and no one wants to not speak, no one wants to look and smile, to accommodate the other. The girl beside me speaks incessantly; she is afraid of seeming dumb. I am content to be dumb, to say nothing that would interest anyone. In a queue for busy bank desks, the man in front and the woman behind me engage each other in conversation, attempt to include me, and I include myself, but no words are said that are listened to, there is only a noise that deadens the silence. I cannot remember anything that was said to me that day. On my way to my parents' house, I see a young boy climbing up a snowy bank, his dog in front of him. "Hi", he calls out, and I answer him, but softly. I walk on. He walks behind me, cheerful, and reiterates his greeting, numerous times, without malice. I turn and smile at him, and at his dog, but say nothing. I do not want to open my mouth. "Hi", he says again; he wants words, noise. I only smile. "Do you not talk?" he says.

43

And everybody lies, nobody uses words the way they want to, nothing is more arduous than effort, simply say what is expected, what will work.

•

But everything, you stupid ass, is a construction, you think only about how things will appear, you wait for her to emerge from the Underground and think not about running to see her, touch her, but about how you should appear, whether the lapel of your coat is elevated appropriately, what she might think of the boots you recently purchased.

•

I must look only, and move, touch, speak with thoughts that are, are not my own, see things I have never, have seen.

44

Finally — whilst sick with influenza — I realise: I want a life of my own. I decide not to contact her that evening, or, rather, to not care about contacting, to not give the act of contact any great weight in the daily decisions about what to do. Adhering to this ruling, I go downstairs, watch *Antiques Roadshow* in the presence of my mother, then turn over to *Top Gear* (where everything is artifice, but how attractive it all is). Then I relent, become bored — is that all it is? — go upstairs, see that she has contacted me, is now away, silently curse — become sad about, whatever that means — her present online absence.

·

I want a life of my own, I want to stand, to not become sad, and how impossible that is here, for there is no balance to the passion, so I am sad, am overwhelmed by it, I want — you are wrong, Patrick — to do more than look on, that is not enough in any business, if you believe that you have no purpose, are not caring, you care still, something, words, capture, touch.

45

In Ireland, I try to remember the virtue — is there not a better word? — of patience, how I had once achieved that difficult state of mind. Then, I think about the results, how I had spent an entire summer thinking I was uninterested, how I had tried to make my mind active, my body passive, take me if you want to, I don't care. How one night, returning from a gallery opening, heading to another bar, another meeting, more drinks, I stood in the middle of a train, looked at a girl who was looking at me, drank slowly and arrogantly from the beer I had been given — no, had taken — some ten minutes before, whilst looking at moving images of a man making strange sounds with his mouth. We looked at each other for a few minutes — there was an honesty, of a sort, about our respective glances — and then I got off somewhere, or she got off somewhere, I can't remember now.

•

In the next bar, I meet friends, and then friends of friends, and then she appears, and we look at each other again, but we do not acknowledge our previous interaction, not even, I believe, implicitly. Someone suggests another venue, and some of us leave, and then, as I am sitting down at another table, another bar, she is there again, only now she is talking, telling us about things, important things, it appears, about her art, about herself, someone — not I — is asking her questions. She says that she can't remember any poetry, yet she learned so much, can anyone here recite any poems, not — she specifies — their own. I deliberately misquote — I would like to think — a short poem by Yeats and, after listening, she says, with a frightening certainty: that's hot.

•

And all people come to Berlin for — all people do anything for — girls and for boys.

46

I think about what will happen after Ireland, this place — being here, in this house — makes me ever more so aware of the idea of the future, makes me worry, makes me consider making money. To not have eyes cast on me, to not have things offered, there is nothing more desirable than, no, it's only a kind of love, can't you see that, can't you simply accept it, but how do you want to make your money, there are many ways to be independent. Being here makes me want to write out words, not speak, so that I can understand what is happening, what has happened, so that my body can relax because I — at last — know it, so that I can then show others that I know it, just so, and then my mind can have clear expression and I can — as she suggested — breathe easy.

•

And who couldn't do with a little bit of romance, a little bit of nonsense, in their life?

47

In Ireland, the question is regularly asked: and what are your plans for next year? Attempting politeness, I smile and say in response: top secret. And then, after each response, I realise what a secret it truly is, for even I have no idea, and I like to forget that fact after I answer each question.

•

And something about being in Ireland makes me bored, and this boredom causes an irritation of my spirit, or my soul, or perhaps I simply need to take some exercise, or masturbate, or drink coffee, or smoke. No, I think, I need to be around bodies and minds that are not angry with themselves.

48

I re-enter a house, go to the coat room, remove my hat, my scarf, my glove. I move to the kitchen and commence preparing my lunch. After a few minutes, someone appears, and gives the whole scene the benefit of his eye and his body. After a moment, he says gently: "D'you want me to peel those carrots for ye?"

"If I wanted you to do it, I would have asked for you to do it."

"All right, all right. I'm only asking."

"I know", I say — breathing — "but there are only so many times you can ask me. Listen to what I'm saying."

•

And all people want, I think, as I catch the eye of a woman later that day, and give her some frivolous lust, is grace, acknowledgement of the beauty of their bodies, accommodation of their ugliness.

49

She tells me what she believes — that she thinks I don't get jealous, that I don't seem that type. But it's not a mastery of emotions, it's not that they don't even exist, it's simply that they are there. I get jealous, I see someone laughing in a photograph, I see a certain physicality between two, certain movements of the body, of the face, smiles which I understand as words, words which mean something else, something I have no understanding of, so I make something up. I do not understand my physicality, our bodies, I do not understand my body, my body, why do our bodies make us sad, that sadness is not common to all, but I am not, in fact, jealous, she is somehow right, that is my philosophy, I repeat it to myself everyday.

•

I see her in what looks a lot like love, bodies in love with each other, and of course it is, they are and why shouldn't I be content with that, bodies happy in their respective symmetry — am I a fantasist? — but then I am reminded of: that night with that other, and the story Jess told me much later, or maybe she told it to me that night, but I forgot, but anyway: she, Jess, left us for a time, sat beside an old drunk, who pointed at us two, sat away from Jess and him and said: there are two people in love, even if they don't even know it, or maybe it was: and they don't even know it, I can't remember for sure.

•

And he was right, I didn't know, for what was there to know, but she made me laugh, I could speak without sense and she understood, or accepted it, even if she didn't understand. She made me think she understood.

•

But how does that translate to a life of contentment? It doesn't, anyway. And then what, I became uncomfortable, for a while I could sleep, I was content, until one morning the sight of her naked and the way in which she clawed at me caused a reaction in my body and I could do no other than leave.

•

Sometimes I think about what Jess told me. I think: maybe I should call her again, no? Then I think of my body and I shudder.

50

And, Sam, you had it wrong, at the wrong time, or in wrong places: Berlin in poverty is preferred to Ireland with riches, or, even, without them.

51

Whilst in Ireland, during the last days there, I get — I think the sight of smoked oysters are involved — to thinking about Melbourne and of her. Images of my time there make their way into my thoughts, and are played out to the theme of some kind of deluded happiness, because I am unhappy, because I have allowed myself to think I have no options of my own to play out, and I have to repeat it to myself, that my time there was not happy, that I was merely content, that everything was safe, there was — however unknown — a future decided, but it was not a decision of my own making, I only wanted to be safe.

But what brought me to the decision to leave, I think again. Imagined slights? What my soul loves, etc.? What were you thinking? Ireland robs me of my faith in my own decision, makes me think — once more — that I was mad to remove myself from all that. Fuck all philosophy. I want money, I want to be safe. No, fuck you, you romanticising, paranoid, weak, body conscious, vain, lazy, fucking prick, get out of here quick, the effect on your body is...

•

I go to Budapest for New Year's Eve, and, in a bar, a man pulls my hair as he walks past me, a prelude to a fight which he wants but which I cannot deliver.

52

And amongst all the detritus of that, she said — black leggings making her legs seem unreal — that she loved me, later that she meant it when she said she loved me, but all I wanted to hear — I'm not even sure if this is real — was how much she loved me better than all the others.

53

She wants, what does she want? We have a conversation at an almost empty bar in Budapest, the kind of place one finds recommended in fashionable guide books, a conversation about intoxication and semantics.

She says: I'm intoxicated by you. And isn't that what you once said to me?

And I say no, what I said was: you are intoxicating, and she said, what's the difference, and I thought, there is one and tried to explain it to her, but she was not convinced.

And now I'm reminded — or is it a premonition I am having — of what the street cleaner said to the composer, upon being asked, well, what should a composer do?

"Well," the street cleaner said, "he should love every note."

•

And people will believe anything that comes out of a good looking mouth, people want to believe it, the old lie, that what they take for beauty equals truth. But even the most beautiful body thinks badly of itself.

54

You want to know what my problem is? I want to do a turn, a number, I want to go on, impersonate, show, represent, I want to tread those precious boards. But I believe myself to be not quite real — it is not a belief — and how, then, would any other believe it, even if feigning?

55

We go dancing. And everybody wants to dance. Everybody. Always. Dancing is what brings them all to joy. That, and listening to the sound of the music. Is it because I won't dance that I have an air of sadness about me? No. The sadness comes from elsewhere. A certain trick I cannot pull off.

•

At the former Hungarian Embassy in Berlin, now a bar, a concert hall, an art space, I stand by a piano and drink an apple juice with vodka while a tall Greek girl of twenty-two talks to me about love, about astrology, about the man whom she loves, who is concentrating on his work at this very moment, who is mixing, listening, thinking about the future. Then she tries to hoist herself up onto the piano, once, no, twice, no, and the third times she makes it, and I see that her underwear is an almost imperceptible pale blue. She rests upon her knees, briefly, the effort of it all a little tiring, and then, standing, she remembers where she is, and starts to shake her hips and torso to the music that her boyfriend is concentrating on creating, and she surveys the crowd assembled all around her.

•

"She looks like she should be selling something," John says.

I motion to her to come closer — that I have something to tell her.

"He says you look like you should be selling something."

"I am," she says, returning to her previous position, and I barely hear what she decides to add: "myself."

56

In bed, on a Monday night, and after a very tiring weekend, I open up my e-mail account and then, without looking at anything contained therein, suddenly think: at what point, and for what reasons, did I start caring about such things again? About the reasons for my tiredness, and my constant desire for mail.

57

I sometimes feel like telling the woman with whom I have recently started to regularly fuck: perhaps we should not have sex the next time we meet, or even, perhaps, the next six times after that. But then she would think I am not a man, or, perhaps more worryingly, that I am somehow not normal.

•

But all forms of human justice and of poetry, it seems, are created in this lull, in the moments when we are too tired or too full of sadness to want to engage with fucking, or even to continue it.

58

When someone turns you down for sex — or even betrays the simple promise of a kiss — on the basis of something they have seen in a second, less distracted glance, something never factored into their initial, obvious attraction and their subsequent, eager offer, well, that, you think, tells you all you need to know.

•

Does it? For people still had sex with you, and, if any slight was created, it was created only by you upon yourself. All were being only honest, either about attraction or a feeling of repugnance. You don't even know how you feel about yourself: sometimes healthily, more often than that you believe yourself famously attractive. Show them what you have got, nothing else, and, more importantly, *hide nothing*.

59

She reads what I write, and she likes it, but — more important — she tells me not to whine and yes, yes, yes, yes — that most courageous of words — she is right.

60

I hear him say, from the comfort of my bedroom, the following words: "beautiful creature", but I have no clear idea to whom he is referring, knowing only that he talks about a girl — of course — and is looking for destruction. He asked me on the U-Bahn for some examples of interesting things to say to a woman, with a view to penetration. While I considered this request I realised that he had discovered that one could quite easily utilise the windows of the train as a mirror.

•

And then I think — for it is with us always — and what, again, is jealousy, and I think, well, it is only a kind of sentimentality, a suffering that we feel, without, perhaps, having suffered, an imposition we make on life of that character who we so often wish to be, if only, I think, because it requires nothing but passivity: the martyr.

61

And then strongly held beliefs start to unravel, but in a quite beautiful way. Collapse is a necessary thing.

62

But only if it is caused by some weakness in one's self. By inadequate architecture. Then, it is a real act of God, caused by none other. A beautiful thing, and quite natural. Such a collapse is caused only by one's self and the remnants will come together to make something that is whole again.

63

I decide to organise an event. I do not quite know why I make this decision, other than that I feel that I must be active. I feel that I must do something, and must be seen to be doing something. The truth — and yet I know it — is that my body is happy doing nothing other than satisfying its desire to continue, and that I am happy being nothing, and that from the moment I commit to the event, to the preparation, the talking, the organisation, I understand that my body is suddenly content — it follows its own bidding — to reject my actions. My body understands that what I am doing is a route to some kind of destruction. A destruction that I have not, in fact, consented to, one imposed by the words and poses of others.

Am I really, I ask myself continually, engaged, engaged in an endeavour to which I have consented? Or did I perhaps dream that this was something that I wanted?

•

And so my chickens come home to roost, or get counted, or some such. Having prevented my body from contenting itself, it illustrates the problem. I get, days before, and on the day, and days after, symptoms of discontent, a pain in my shoulder, a throbbing in the right hand side of my skull, an inability to talk, a dissatisfaction with my gait, with words, with the simple action of listening.

My body, in fact, turns itself off.

•

And at the event, I ask about the original photographer, whose name we do not — may never — know, who is not here to present her — or his — role in the proceedings, whose name — it becomes apparent — is not even of interest to you and all I can remember thinking is: what are you? Merely an eager curator of images, taken by other people? A collector, yes, but not — no — a maker. You only ever lifted your finger to press "buy". You consume the things that speak to you with beauty, and then you make presents of them.

64

Repulsion — a certain type of gaze, when one sees something that one does not consider as being entirely within the realm of what one has decided is possible, and therefore also not beautiful — is inevitable. A condition caused, largely, by lack of imagination.

•

Cutting a chilli pepper, for example, as I have always cut chilli peppers — as I have cut other small and delicate things, garlic, for example, which I crush with my stump before peeling off the skin, or walnuts, or the smallest granules of aromatic sea salt — that is to say: without injury, the injury is already done, I can feel, but not yet see, the gaze, it always comes, and perhaps with it, later, a comment. The viewer — used to televised productions, movie stills, the advertisements of fashion magazines — begins to consider the certain type of distaste that they are feeling for what it is they see. It is not in the realm of their experience, it is not usual and therefore it is not something they believe they want to see, it is not, therefore, good, it does not embody their body, and it is certainly neither pretty nor even simply attractive, they probably begin to think: an injury will be done. They, you see, knowing only their own body, and others like it, know better.

•

But the injury is there, it is not any potential for disaster that brings forth comment, it is not concern, it is the disaster already there that disquiets their eyes, if I were a petty man I would say: it is simply the fact that they can see it and it is perhaps touching a vegetable, something they are very likely to later have to put into their mouths.

•

Some of the photographs shown at the event I organise are in fact found photographs of criminals, people convicted for crimes such as running away and running numbers, he who shows them imagines one woman incapable of having committed any crime — he does not know, perhaps, that these things are so often simply about the numbers, or the boredom of officials, of course not all crimes are crimes — because of the so much decency he can see in her particular face, and that face has skin of a darker colour, and therefore she must have been — he imagines (likes to?) — subject to a particular inequity of justice. It must now only be good, and emphatically maligned, that face, just as it once could only be bad, and unequal to any virtue. That face is now for him incapable of being the multitude of confused things that constitute a life.

•

Why is it that we think our own bodies so good, so rigidly defined, incapable of contradiction, other bodies so much only like our own?

•

And look, look on, what is it to me, I return to those first indignant words with which I replied, and to my indignant spirit, I am also a thing of God, and am natural, under the aspect of eternity I exist and have striven, have endeavoured to survive, without the benefit of symmetry. What, in fact, have you done?

65

And then, again, always again, you think: you need to sort yourself out, whatever that means, but those are the words you use, the words that are voiced by someone in your head. Sort yourself out, look after yourself, that is the sensible thing to do, and all this, you think, again, in bed with a beautiful woman, a woman who loves you, you think. I can do without all of this, without her worries, her worries about who I am, about how we compare. Why do we let the standard of another worry us about how we should be — because we have no imagination. And then, somehow you think about the life you had created with her, which was, in a sense, absolutely sorted, a comfortable life, a good life, with regular income, good weather, healthy food, and the ability to read the newspaper every Saturday, in English, and how nice was that? You give in to the story of that love together and, of course, you feel sad, but you are simply experiencing current difficulties, it is the practical happiness that you miss, and you don't even miss that. Is this at all reasonable? And then you think: and who gives a fuck about reason. Did you ever do anything, Benedict? Did you ever even leave the fucking house?

•

What wouldn't we all give to be forever busy, to be always going to another interview, the subject of which was only ever our self.

66

And what was it with organising, with thinking in abstractions, that made you think you were beginning to go a little mad? Not that there is anything wrong with a little madness now and again.

•

The necessity for a strange type of exactitude in everything, other than in art: dealing with impossibility. No wonder you felt a strain on your senses.

67

We decide to go to a club. It has the reputation of being difficult to get into. It was a Saturday, we were at a party, just the two of us, she had finished performing and I, uncharacteristically, suddenly felt like dancing but, of course, to different music, music somewhat like the music they were playing but of course different, in a very subtle way. My phone rang at that very moment. It was a friend, someone not unknown for going out dancing by himself on Saturday nights until the very early morning. What am I up to? Would I like to join him elsewhere? At this club? I relay the suggestion to her and she agrees: we will go to the monolithic building.

•

She wants to see me dance and to dance with me, or for me, or some such. She has made these desires very clear. I am suddenly aware that I don't feel very comfortable about satisfying her request, about dancing together. I feel that there is something unreal in all of what is now happening, but something in me accedes. Whatever bodily mechanism is used for self-preservation, whatever muscle or nerve or bone or cell moves me constantly towards existing and away from shame, from lack of dignity, moroseness and stuttering idiocy, it fails me that night. In other words: my mind is thinking only of impressing her.

•

There is a large and powerful strobe light in the main room of the club and while walking through this main hall, to get to another section of the building, I close my eyes to diminish the effect. We reach our destination, and begin to dance. Someone comes up and whispers "du bist wunderschön" to her. I'm trying to forget about the effect of the strobe light, I'm trying to dance but it's not, somehow, working as it should. I go to the bar to order a drink and, while sitting on a stool, a girl bumps into me, she is wearing a hat and has coloured stars upon her face. She talks to me in German and tumbles into me again as she tries to take her seat.

"What are you drinking?"

"A lemonade."

"That's very innocent. You're very innocent."

I turn to my friend, now seated beside me and find that I cannot talk anymore, there is a pain in the muscle which allows my mouth to move, and a pain in the right hand side of my head every time a word is uttered.

"I've got to go", I say, without explanation, and then, somehow, I manage to repeat it as I get up to leave: "I've got to go."

68

And now I remember — am reminded of, rather, but by what? — the mornings, the mornings from Queens Parade to Plenty Road, and how I must have thought — but did I? — all of this might last forever.

69

I went all the way there to see her. I changed a flight to arrive early, to surprise. No, not completely true, I remember feeling terribly alone upon an island in Malaysia, a man at a port there said, where are you from, and I said, Ireland, and he said, Ireland, aaaahh — with great delight — and what are you doing out here then, as if my presence there was the stupidest thing in the world. I phoned her up from a payphone in North Melbourne and she was at her father's house, watching a movie. She drove in to collect me and we went to have a drink somewhere, I can't remember the name of that bar, but I do remember that I drank two — or maybe it was three? — vodkas with some apple juice in very quick succession.

•

Some days later we met for lunch and it was only then that I realised, yes, what was it you realised? That you expect too much, that others can live their lives and offer love. That you didn't understand that then. That all you wanted was love, a world only of love, because you refused to accept the world as it was, but that was understandable, no? You had certainly good reason to ignore things, to desire, what was that word you repeated to yourself? Sanctuary. Anyway, at lunch you realised that it had perhaps been a bad idea to do all the things that you had done, that she did — indeed — have her own life, she had no need — no need such as you had — to constantly look elsewhere, that she had — no wonder — connected to that again, whereas you had no life, you were constantly looking, and so adrift, and so you saw all that in her eyes, or she saw it in yours and you saw that and you cursed your stupid actions.

•

All in good faith, not at all wasted. You persevered. You adapted, undermined — as always — your own desires and wishes, or didn't even know what they were, so used were you to modifying yourself to the satisfaction of others.

•

And two years later you, having established a life together, having convinced yourself of the saving grace of your love for another, are reminded of how much you still hate yourself, still hate yourself, and thus some others, and thus some other things, and you see only persecution, difficulty, and demeaning strength and happiness everywhere.

•

You — there are only two words for it — withdraw and then you flee.

70

Someone planted a flower between the floorboards in my room the other night, during a party held in honour of the birthday of my flatmate. A woman from Finland, she took an artificial leaf from my desk, anointed it a flower, and inserted it into the gap between the boards.

•

Across from that, a pretty woman from Portugal sat by the small, round table with her friend and looked bored. She produced, halfway through the evening, an ornate fan, and, extending it fully, proceeded to alleviate her ennui by vigorously cooling her face. Admittedly, the room was very warm that night.

•

At some point, Martin disappeared, returning minutes later with the fan, which he, too, proceeded to aggressively air his face with. He looked at me, winking, or, at least, so I imagined.

•

All of this occurred some time after a performance which I also attended that evening, a performance that I left immediately after it had finished, because I wanted to quickly make my way to the birthday party and avoid being too late. The performers were her, and Marty. When they later arrived at the party they found a corner of the room absent of people and she produced two little bottles of Jägermeister, which, after having been properly distributed, they proceeded to quickly neck.

•

And then I saw her whispering to Darko, and imagined later that she might have pointed out the boots she had left in the corner of the room, behind the sofa, because on the way to the bar he says:

"Boots, do you like boots?" —

to which I reply, yes, and then he pointed to Saana, the Finnish girl, who I then noticed had two black earrings in one ear and one black earring in the other, and he said:

"You must like her boots, then..."

— to which I reply, no, I prefer them with heels, and then he said:

"You like to be stepped on..."

and then I laughed and laughed and almost said — not that it would have mattered — yes.

71

And he — some other — said:

"Well, we've been orbiting each other for some time now, haven't we?"

— even if I wasn't there to hear it, but it made me think of those nights when we believe, somehow, we've got a chance at something, and the words we then decide we have to use.

"All those nights at the ping pong bar..."

he said — so she said to me —

"Looking... Cleopatra-like."

72

And she can feel sad, of course, even sadder because no one answers their phone at 10.30 on a Tuesday night, no one is available to distract her from this sadness, from her feelings that she, what, that she exists and that she doesn't?

•

And I can worry about the constancy of her mind, having seen her very happy hours before the sadness, but how much do I fool myself with my own certainties, or ignore my infidelity to the words that I give out at certain times.

73

Not that any of this matters. Desire, that appears to matter, wanting to enchant someone else — powerful — or to be enchanted — ecstatically powerless. A constant supply of satisfiable wants. And easy hatred, caused by failing to eat at the appropriate time and not understanding that. The result: a pornographic philosophy and supplication using curse words.

74

Gamal tells me — tells everyone — that what he writes constitutes a revenge on the world, his writing does so, my writing does so, the best writing should do so. Maybe there is some truth in that, or was, in the way I lived, but now I think: no, I do not want revenge.

•

I did want it, it would have been stupid to pretend otherwise — perhaps I did that also — but to whom would I have inflicted my hate? The world, as he says? I can still write without hating the world.

75

The other day, while out walking with her, while looking for a place suitable to eat lunch at — lunch as a treat to her, after she had done me a favour, after she had accompanied me to an administrative office, to wait patiently with me while I waited to sort out an administrative matter — I saw a young man emerge from a door that faced onto the street and was in some way struck — otherwise I would not be writing about it now, but I in no way know what I exactly mean by struck — by an expression on his face of what I came to read as sadness, as if — as if I knew — he had just received some terrible news, that very minute previous, from a loved one or from a relative, or from what is both, a loved relative, as if that terrible news was information of the end of the relationship with that person, resulting from, perhaps, the promise of their death or from other, unknown means.

For the remainder of our walk — we eventually were successful in finding a lunch venue, where I had onion soup and chicken salad — I could think only of the news he might have received, had such a thing occurred, of the face of the one — so dear to him — who told him of it.

•

The faint but lingering smell of chocolate scented body lotion on the sheets of my bed made me write this.

76

I read about a model who tried to commit suicide, a beautiful woman who was, by her own account, in love, in love with some idea of love, of how her life should be, the right thing to do.

The world and other people in it moved on, her life distracted itself from what she had thought, it looked around, and she was left with only her body, without exercise, too full of alcohol, and she probably wondered, so I like to imagine to myself: what happened to that vision that I had, to those words with which I convinced myself that everything would be ok?

She had forgotten to satisfy the demands of her body. She had distanced herself from his, but still, understandably, dreamed of it and her body together.

•

The result can take many forms: an urge to smoke more cigarettes than one normally does, a period of life after which one wonders *where was I then?*, constant worry, an inability to focus on the present.

•

But I don't know the specifics that led her to that love, I don't know the words, the smells, caresses, looks, that made her feel beautiful and without which there is no love, before we talk about anything

that is real and truly meant.

77

I start crying whilst taking a shower, the moment the hot water wets my hair and runs down my face it causes — so I believe — a reaction, my body relaxes and I cry in a way that I find both necessary and satisfying.

•

She invites me to a ball, something in London, a city where I used to live but now find too dense with people. Any decision to attend is not one that I find I can make instantly. I cannot say to myself: I want to go, or even, with equal certainty: I do not want to go. I think about my body. My body seems to determine my response, any possibility of a response. I think about the reactions of children to a television presenter who has only one hand. She frightens the children, some mothers report. The presenter emanates a calmness concerning all of this that I believe to be false.

•

And, the next morning, a sense of perspective is felt — and thanks for this is given to something — light emerges once more, motion continues outside the window of my room, I find — I knew it anyway, I like to think — that I can be moved to happiness again. The alarm on my new mobile phone goes off, I am caused to think of life in Tokyo by the music and the colors and typography as I look to turn the phone off. I think of the taste of my favorite Japanese food:

fish, with eggs still inside, fried until crispy, cooked rice shaped into the form of a triangle and warm sake.

78

I miss, I will miss, I do miss [the details of a life are what constitute a life]. Sadness is O.K. I am sad. I am tired. It is very early, 6.30 a.m. on a Monday morning and she gets out of bed to go to the airport to get on a flight to England. I think that I am going to feel very alone, then thinking about that makes me believe that no, I will not. It is dark outside. No doubt it is very cold [it is February].

•

I start to think about the idea of specifics. I try to imagine the different specifics.

•

Shane Anderson, an American living in Berlin, wakes up at 4.53 a.m. on Tuesday morning and before waking, consciousness makes him realise that he is very thirsty, before memory causes him to link that thirst to the apple juice he bought the evening before at the Kaiser's on the corner of Kottbusser Tor (terrible alliteration, he thinks to himself, a writer could do better, but it is early he then thinks, and my god I'm thirsty, he thinks), before he steels himself to lift his body off the double mattress that he bought at IKEA near Südkreuz, before he goes to the small fridge (refrigerator, he says out loud and smiles to himself) and lifts the clear apple juice out of the fridge (refrigerator, he says once more) and pours the little remaining into a small clear glass someone gifted to him as one of a pair on his 25th birthday, he thinks: the one thing I must do today, must, must, is write a message thanking everybody for coming to the reading last night.

79

Still in Berlin, the man at the corner store bags, for me, the bottle of apple juice and the bottle of sparkling water, offers me the handles of the bag with a gentleness and with the beginnings of, so I think, a smile, this the man who John and I decided was not at all as friendly as the other man, the one who ran the shop across the road.

Which makes me think of something a philosopher once wrote, his name isn't that important, something like, you can't disagree with a thing just because it's not presented in the tone you would prefer. You can't disagree with such things, perhaps he was right, but you can avoid them as much as is possible.

•

Apart from that:

Marguerite Eliaszadeh, Iranian, American, British and tall, poured cheap red wine from a bottle that had been bought two hours previously at Penny Markt, a supermarket located only five minutes from her front door and which she had never noticed the existence of prior to Wednesday of that week, during when (after lunch?) a visiting friend pointed it out to her, discovered in his own way [furtive attendance there in order to buy a packet of condoms on recommendation of the woman he was visiting in a flat across the way]; she poured cheap red wine into a tall and delicate wine glass, the colour and sound of the liquid dropping out of one container and into another reminding her of a wedding she had attended some years earlier, in Bromley, during which her ex-girlfriend had rather pointedly referred to her, while talking loudly to a mutual friend at the bar while buying shots, as her ex-wife. She smiled at the memory, and tasted the wine.

80

And then who do you think but Zadie Smith, she wakes up too, in Rome, in a room that makes her think — at least it did the night before, but then she was a little drunk — of Burt Lancaster in *The Leopard*, the presence of her husband in the bed evidenced by the slight sound of another person breathing, this she notices because she is absolutely still, she faces the wall that allows her to avoid a view of him and then she thinks only of the following once she has satisfied herself [she has not yet seen him since the night before] that he is still there and he is still breathing: and what will I write about today?

•

Hold on, no, no, no. These are all stories for well-adjusted people, whatever that means. I am not that, I think. I am the cause for worry. I cannot empathise at all because I am thinking only of myself and also of not spending any money.

81

Maybe this:

Charlie Sheen wakes up after one hour and twenty minutes sleep, after lying down on his bed — a gift from his father, Martin, who played Captain Willard in *Apocalypse Now* (who killed Brando, for God's sake, [Charlie think to himself.] Did I really say that yesterday to that guy from TMZ.com? What is wrong with me?) — at 4 a.m. and thinks, thinks, thinks, what do I want, how to start the day in a way that will make me believe that it will be a goddamn good one: yes, he wants some coffee, he thinks, half pre-made — those fucks from Warner Bros., what fucking assholes, now I have to deal with all this shit, now I can't get any fucking sleep — half instant.

A goddess walks past the open door of the bedroom. A goddess. Why goddesses, the guy from TMZ asked me yesterday, didn't he? Why goddesses? What did I say, you ask questions to which you already know the answers, something like that, to which the answers should be obvious. Goddess looks, brain melts. Charlie fucking Sheen. What a bitchin' name.

Charlie gets off the bed which his father gave him and walks into the bathroom, a walk during which he shouts out, to nobody in particular [although his request will be heard and almost instantly satisfied], "can I get a half and half, no fuckin' water in the instant, just mix 'em."

A. Real. Fucking. Intellectual bender. These last few days, yeah. What a fucking rock star I am, yeah, Jesus my neck looks like that of a much older man.

82

Is that enough?

•

When it was all over for me, when I wanted, without knowing it — when my body wanted — to no longer function, I thought that I — my body — relished such a possibility, or was, at least, prepared for it.

You must think: you thought not feeling was a good thing. Not that I was attempting not to feel. A reaction was occurring within my body and I felt that — perhaps it was even a function of the laws of physics — I could not feel good about myself.

•

People only like people — are prepared to tolerate them — when they accede to their idea of what they want them to be.

Talk back then, and see how long it is before they say: I think we are talking about this too much.

•

And I don't understand it but I am uncomfortable with acts that require me — Require? What a word! — to... well, here:

She — Who is she? The mother of the cat? — her name is Sara, Sara organises, by way of simple e-mails and in the most preliminary way and only with a view to the merest possibility of something actually happening, totally dependent on my mood on the actual day, a kind of party, not even a party, the merest kind of gathering.

What could be more considerate?

What could I have been more in need of?

•

Something, given.

83

I am thinking still of Sheen and now also of Galliano, of course these events are nothing new, as John said, of course not, and nothing new lies behind them, and nothing new is in them, they are not even events, if one looks on a website, finds something of interest relating to a person one has met, or seen, and translates that something from German into a sentence that reads: terminated because of psychological problems its career, how does that help with understanding any of it?

•

So I have a drink, a reaction to that scary — yes — feeling — yes — when you feel that life is somehow slipping by when they are not around.

•

He felt a strange type of sadness on Wednesday night, as a result of which he decided to finish off the bottle of wine left in the kitchen by a friend of his the night before she flew away on an airplane, he talks with his sister on Skype, she tells him that she is about to go for a walk around the town, a bit of exercise, his flatmate returns to the flat after having been at an art gallery where a poet whom he, flatmate, has published the work of was performing a cabaret, they decide to go a bar to meet some Portuguese friends, at which bar pool is played by almost all, at which bar he decides that now he does not feel sad any more, at which bar he has a beer, after which beer they all leave, after which leaving she gets into a car and drives off, after which driving off he thinks about her shoes, after such a thought he and his flatmate walk home and after which walking home all go to bed.

He felt a strange type of sadness on Wednesday night. By the next morning it had left him.

84

Better. Or, time has passed without any of the horrible incidents I constantly worry about happening.

85

I sit in bed, imagine fog having the character of water, delicately put my toe into fog as I would into water and then, satisfied, my body follows.

86

I consider videotaping myself masturbating so that I can post the results on this website, *beautiful agony*, where only the faces of those reaching sexual orgasm are shown. The viewer of these videos knows nothing about who is doing what to these people, is it just themselves or is there someone else involved?

I like the idea of showing my face, not being expected to show my body.

•

And how can I come up with thoughts such as: it's a strange person that would have sex with a man with one hand.

•

I don't like to be subject to such as you.

•

But people do not — not always — not all people — think or see as you do.

And you can charm, of course, but you can not control how it is that other people see you, can you even understand that they can see you?

•

This, love, and if it must, its end.

87

John brought home a bag the other day, a bag emblazoned, one might say, with the Union Jack, a bag given to him by the Portuguese to carry books in, to which bag I had a reaction, a reaction predetermined only by an accident of birth. Write what's in your blood Joyce said, but write this:

I called it the butcher's apron, he said he liked the color of the blue.

•

And Sara wrote, underneath all this the question of homecoming and escape, and I think of people who love and do not judge when no judgment is necessary and people who hate only and judge always because of fear of water-like fog and to which my response should always be the same and requires me to think of how they view me and

•

And can I now get out of my bed and tick off the things I have written on my list of things to do today and then go to the shop and buy something to eat, something that I love? And I suppose I should say that I am beginning to feel some kind of

•

Sleep in their bed if it makes you feel safe, if they let you.

Carry a sentimental ring of theirs in your pocket, for unknown reasons, accidentally leave it on tables while eating food with others, do not be embarrassed to pick it up upon discovery and declare, without words, only with the grace and openness of the action, yes, an object so incongruous to your image has something to do with you.

And talk to friends, and sleep in their beds, if they let you, and carry their rings too.

88

Outside, the light of the sun.

89

Outside, the city of Berlin.